Leo Tols.
*and* P.

Twenty-two Russian Tales
for Young Children
by Leo Tolstoy

# Twenty-two Russian Tales for Young Children by Leo Tolstoy

Selected, Translated, and with an Afterword by
*MIRIAM MORTON*

Illustrated by Eros Keith

Simon and Schuster, New York

*To Caroline*
M.M.

FIRST PRINTING

SBN 671-65072-6 Trade
SBN 671-65073-4 Library
Library of Congress Catalog Card Number: 70-84139
Manufactured in the United States of America

# CONTENTS

## Stories

## Fables and Fairy Tales

STORIES

# Philipok

There once was a boy named Philip. Because he was still so small, everyone called him Philipok. One day when his brothers and sisters were leaving for school, he put on his cap and started to go with them. But his mother said:

"Where are you off to, Philipok?"

"To school."

"You're still too young for school, Philipok. You must stay home."

The older children left. Their father had gone early that morning to his job in the forest. Now their mother left to do housework for a wealthy neighbor. Philipok remained alone with his grandmother.

The grandmother was very old; as usual, she was now asleep in the corner over the stove. Philipok was lonesome and bored. He looked for his cap. He couldn't find it. He put on his father's old one and set out for school by himself.

The schoolhouse was at the far end of the village, near the church. When Philipok walked down his own street, the dogs didn't bother him—they knew him. But later, as he was passing the houses of strangers, several dogs rushed out at him from their yards. One of them was huge. They were all running after him and barking. Philipok ran away. The dogs ran after him, barking harder than ever. Philipok screamed, stumbled, and fell.

A man came out, chased the dogs away, and said to the little boy, "Where are you going all by yourself, little one?"

Philipok didn't answer him, but lifted the sides of his long coat and ran as fast as his legs would carry him. He ran all the way to the schoolhouse. There was no one in sight on the porch, but he could hear the voices of the children reading their lessons out loud inside the schoolroom. Philipok felt scared. "What if the teacher chases me away?" he thought. He didn't know what to do now. If he went back home, he'd be chased by those dogs. But he was also afraid of the teacher.

Just then a woman carrying a pail of water walked past the school. She saw Philipok and said to him, "The other children are inside, learning. Why are you wasting your time out here?"

Philipok went inside. He removed his cap in the hall and opened the door to the schoolroom. It was full of children. They were talking and shouting. The teacher, wearing a red muffler, was pacing up and down between the rows of tables.

"What do you want?" he asked Philipok in a stern voice.

The little boy clutched his cap and said nothing.

"Who are you?"

He kept silent.

"Have you lost your tongue?"

Philipok was so frightened by now that he couldn't utter a word.

"Go on home if you don't want to speak," the teacher said.

The little boy would have gladly said something, but his throat was dry from fright. He stared at the teacher and began to cry. The teacher felt sorry for Philipok. He patted his head and asked the children who he was.

The children cried, "It's Philipok, Kostushkin's little brother." "He always begs to go to school." "His mother wouldn't let him." "Now he has come on the sly."

"In that case, little one, go sit down on that bench, next to your brother. I'm going to ask your mother to let you come to school from now on," the teacher said.

Then he began to show Philipok his ABC's, but the little boy already knew all the letters. He could even read a little.

"Now tell me how you spell your name," said the teacher.

Looking down bashfully at his feet and stammering, Philipok hastily spelled his name, as if he were afraid that the letters would run away if he didn't hurry.

The class burst out laughing.

"Good boy!" said the teacher. "Tell me, who taught you all this?"

Feeling bolder now, Philipok blurted out, "My brother Kostushka. I am a clever one, I learn fast. I am terribly smart!"

The teacher laughed and said, "Don't be in such a hurry to sing your own praises. Study a while first."

From that day on, Philipok came to school with his brothers and sisters.

# The Two Friends

Once two friends were walking in the woods. A bear
jumped out at them. One of the men ran away, climbed a tree, and
hid himself in its branches. The other remained where he was, fell to the
ground, and pretended to be dead.

The bear came closer and smelled him. The man didn't even breathe. The bear
smelled his face, thought him dead, and went away.

When the beast was out of sight, the man in the tree came down, laughing.

"Tell me," he said to his friend, "what did the bear whisper into your ear?"

"He said that it is a cowardly person who runs away when his friend is in danger."

# The Old Man
# and the Apple Trees

A very old man was planting apple trees. His neighbors said to him:

"Why are you bothering to plant these trees? It will be a long time before they bear fruit, and you will not live to taste even one little apple."

The old man replied:

"I will not get to eat any of the apples, but others will and they will thank me."

# The Trapped Bird

It was Sergei's birthday. He got many gifts that day—stuffed teddy bears, toy ponies, picture books. But the gift he liked best was the cage for trapping birds that his uncle gave him.

There was a small, flat board attached to the opening on the side of the cage. When seeds were scattered on this board and a bird came to peck at them, the board would snap shut, and the bird would be trapped in the cage. Sergei happily showed the cage to his mother.

"That is not a nice toy!" she said. "Why do you want to trap birds? Why torment them?"

"I'll only catch them in the cage," said Sergei. "They'll sing and I'll feed them."

So the little boy found some seeds, scattered them on the small board, and placed the cage in the garden. He stood near it, waiting for the birds to come. But the birds were afraid of him and didn't go near the cage. Sergei went into the house to eat his dinner. He left the cage outside. After his meal, he came out again into the garden, looked at the cage, and saw a little bird trapped in it. He was glad. He picked up the bird in his hand, and carried it into the house.

"Mamma, look! I caught a bird! It's probably a nightingale! My, how its heart beats!"

"It's a finch," said the mother. "Be sure not to hurt it. Better let it go free."

"No, I'll keep it, and give it food and water."

Sergei put the little finch back into the cage. And for the next two days he remembered to take care of it. On the third day, he forgot all about the finch and didn't change its water.

"You see," his mother said to him, "you forgot to take care of your bird. Better let it go."

"No. I won't forget again. I'll give it some fresh water right away, and I'll clean the cage."

Sergei stuck his hand inside the cage and began to clean it. The bird was frightened and beat its wings against the cage, trying to keep out of the way of Sergei's hand. The boy finished cleaning the cage. Now he went to get the water. His mother saw that he had forgotten to close the cage door.

"Sergei, close the cage," she cried, "or your bird will get out and kill itself!"

She had barely said this when the little finch found the opening, and, happy to gain its freedom, spread its little wings and flew quickly across the room, straight to the window. The bird didn't see the glass, struck against it hard with its little body, and fell to the windowsill.

Sergei came running. He lifted the bird and carried it back to the cage. It was still alive, but it lay on its little chest, its wings limp, and breathed heavily. Sergei looked and looked at it and began to cry.

"Mamma, what should I do now?"

"Now there is nothing you can do."

Sergei didn't leave the cage all day. He kept looking at the little finch. The bird lay there on its chest, its little sides heaving. When Sergei went to bed that evening, the bird was still alive. He couldn't fall asleep for a long time. Whenever he closed his eyes, he would see the little bird lying in its cage, breathing painfully.

In the morning, when Sergei went over to the cage, he saw that the bird was now lying stiffly on its back, its little feet crossed. It was dead. After that Sergei never again wanted to trap birds.

# A Boy Tells the Story
# of Being Caught
# in a Storm

When I was a small boy, I was sent to the woods one day to gather some mushrooms. I went into the woods, picked a kerchief-full of mushrooms, and started home. Suddenly the sky grew dark, and it began to rain and to thunder. I was scared and sat down under a big oak tree. The lightning kept flashing; it was so bright that it hurt my eyes, and I closed them. Over my head something cracked and crashed, and then something hit me.

I fell over and lay there stunned until it stopped raining. When I came to, the trees were dripping, the birds were singing, and the sun was shining on everything.

The big oak tree had been struck by the lightning and smoke was coming from its stump. There were lots of chips from the tree all around me. My clothes were wringing wet and stuck to my body. I had a big lump on my head, and it hurt. I found my cap, picked up my mushrooms, and ran home.

There was no one in the house. I cut myself a piece of bread and ate it, then I curled up on the bench near the stove. When I woke up, I smelled fried mushrooms—there, on the table, was a bowl full of them, and everyone was eating. I cried, "Why are you eating without me!" And they said, "Why are you lying there, sleepyhead? Hurry up, come and eat."

# Rusak's Night Frolic

[*In Russia, the large gray hare whose color does not change is called "Rusak."*]

In the winter, Rusak lived near a village. One night, he raised one floppy ear and listened; he raised the other floppy ear, twitched his whiskers, sniffed the air, and sat down on his hind legs. Then he leaped once or twice over the deep snow, again sat down, and looked around. There was no one and nothing to be seen anywhere, except snow. The snow lay in waves and glistened, like sugar. Overhead there was a frosty mist, and big bright stars peeped through it.

Rusak was on his way to the threshing barn in the village. He had to cross a wide road to get there. He could hear, coming from this busy road, the whoosh of sleigh runners, the neighing of horses, and the creaking of heavily loaded sledges.

The hare took a few more leaps and stopped at the edge of the road. He now saw the peasants walking alongside their sledges, the collars of their cloaks raised high. Their beards, moustaches, and eyebrows were white with frost, and steam poured from their mouths and nostrils. The horses' hides were sweaty; the cold had turned the sweat to hoarfrost. The horses were pushing each other with their harness collars. Sometimes they stumbled, then scrambled out of the ruts in the road. Some peasants ran after the horses, caught up with them, and urged them on with their whips. Two old peasants were walking side by side; one was telling the other that his horse had been stolen.

When the string of sledges had passed, Rusak leaped across the road and slowly made his way toward the threshing barn. A small dog who had been following the sledges noticed him. The dog barked and streaked after Rusak. The hare hopped over the snowdrifts. He managed to stay on top of the drifts, but the dog sank into the snow on his tenth jump and gave up the chase. Seeing this, Rusak stopped to rest a while, then quietly continued his journey. On the way, in the wheat field, he met two other hares. They were nibbling and frisking about. Rusak played with his friends, dug with them in the snow, ate some winter grain, and went on. The village was hushed; all the lights were out. On the street could be heard only the sound of a crying baby coming from inside one of the huts and the creaking of timber from the frost.

Rusak finally reached the threshing barn. He found other friends there. He played with them on the bare threshing floor, helped himself to some oats from an opened bushel basket, climbed up to the snow-covered roof of the barn, squeezed through the wattle fence, and started home to his dell.

It was beginning to grow light now. Fewer stars could be seen in the sky, and the frosty mist lay heavier over the ground. The village was waking. The women were coming out to fetch water, the men were bringing fodder from the barns, the children were whining and crying. There were even more sledges and sleighs on the road now, and there was much loud talking among the drivers.

Rusak hopped quickly across the road. He went to where his old burrow was, picked out a new spot, a little higher on the slope, dug away the snow, and huddled on his haunches in his new burrow. He flattened his ears over his back and fell asleep, with his eyes open.

# The Peasant and the Horse

One day a peasant had to take his loaded wagon across the river. There was a raft nearby. The peasant unharnessed the horse and pushed the wagon onto the raft; but the horse was stubborn and would not get on the raft. The peasant pulled the horse by the bridle with all his might—he pulled and he pulled, but he couldn't make the horse move. So he tried to push the animal onto the raft from the back, but it wouldn't budge.

Then the peasant had an idea: he would pull the horse by its tail *away* from the river. The horse was still stubborn and refused to go where its master was now pulling it. Instead it walked in the other direction, straight onto the raft.

# The King
# and the Humble Hut

A king built himself a new palace. A garden was planted around it. At the very entrance to the garden stood a humble hut, where a poor peasant lived. The king wanted the hut to be torn down so that it would not spoil the beauty of his garden. He called his minister and told him to buy the hut from the peasant.

The minister went to the peasant and said to him, "You are lucky! The king wants to buy your hut. It isn't worth even ten rubles, but he is offering you one hundred."

"No, I won't sell the hut for a hundred," said the peasant.

"Then here is two hundred."

"I won't sell it for two hundred or even for a thousand. My grandfather and my father lived in this hut and died in this hut, and I grew old in it and shall die in it, God willing."

The minister returned to the king.

"That peasant is stubborn," he said to the king. "He will not take any price for his

ugly hut. King, don't give him anything for it—just order that it be torn down, and that will be that."

"No, I shall do no such thing," said the king.

The minister said, "Then what is to be done? How can you allow the ugly hut to remain right across from your new palace! People will look at the palace and say, 'A fine palace, but the hut spoils everything. It seems that the king didn't have enough money to buy the hut.'"

The king said, "No, those who look at the palace will say, 'Of course the king had to have a lot of money to build such a palace.' And when they see the humble hut, they will say, 'But the king also has a good heart.' Let the peasant stay in his humble hut."

# The Old Grandfather and His Little Grandson

The grandfather had become very old. His legs would not carry him, his eyes could not see, his ears could not hear, and he was toothless. When he ate, bits of food sometimes dropped out of his mouth. His son and his son's wife no longer allowed him to eat with them at the table. He had to eat his meals in the corner near the stove.

One day they gave him his food in a bowl. He tried to move the bowl closer, it fell to the floor and broke. His daughter-in-law scolded him. She told him that he spoiled everything in the house and broke their dishes, and she said that from now on he would get his food in a wooden dish. The old man sighed and said nothing.

A few days later, the old man's son and his wife were sitting in their hut, resting and watching their little boy playing on the floor. They saw him putting together something out of small pieces of wood. His father asked him, "What are you making, Misha?"

The little grandson said, "I'm making a wooden bucket. When you and Mamma get old, I'll feed you out of this wooden dish."

The young peasant and his wife looked at each other and tears filled their eyes. They were ashamed because they had treated the old grandfather so meanly, and from that day they again let the old man eat with them at the table and took better care of him.

# The Eagle

An eagle built a nest in a tree beside a busy road, far from the sea, and hatched several baby eagles.

One day, when the eagle returned to the nest with a large fish in her claws, there were men working nearby. Seeing the fish, they surrounded the tree, shouting and throwing stones at the eagle. When the eagle dropped her fish, they picked it up and went away.

The eagle perched on the edge of the nest, and the eaglets raised their little heads and cheeped and shrilled. They were hungry. But their mother was too tired to fly back to the sea. She lowered herself into the nest, covered her babies with her wings, petted them and smoothed their feathers, as though begging them to be patient. But the more she petted them the louder they squawked and shrilled.

The eagle left them and perched on a higher branch.

The eaglets kept shrilling even more pitifully.

Suddenly the mother eagle gave a desperate cry, spread her wings, and flew wearily toward the sea.

She returned late in the evening, flying slowly and low, again bringing in her claws a large fish.

As she swooped toward the nest she looked down to see if there were any people near the tree. Seeing none, she folded her wings and perched on the edge of the nest. The eaglets raised their little heads and opened their little beaks. Their mother tore off pieces of the fish and fed her hungry babies.

# The Kitten

Once there were a brother and a sister. The brother's name was Vasya, the sister was called Katya. They had a cat. In the spring their cat was lost. The children looked for her everywhere, but they couldn't find her. One day, when Vasya and Katya were playing near the barn, they heard a soft miaow from somewhere above them. Vasya climbed the ladder to the hayloft, Katya waited below, asking, "Is she there? Have you found her?"

At first Vasya didn't answer, then he called down to her, "I found her! It's our cat. . . . She has kittens! Such cute ones! Come up, quick!"

Katya ran home first, got some milk, and brought it for the cat.

There were five kittens. When they grew a little bigger and began to crawl out of the corner where they had been born, the children chose one for themselves, gray with white paws, and carried it to the house. Their mother gave the other four away, but let the children keep the gray-and-white one. They fed it, played with it, and took it to bed with them at night.

One day Vasya and Katya went to play on the road and took their kitten with them.

There was a lively breeze which blew about bits of straw on the road. The kitten played with the stirring bits of straw as though they were mice. The children laughed. Then they found some dandelions beside the road. They began to pick them, forgetting all about their kitten.

Suddenly they heard someone shout, "Come back, come back!" It was a hunter on horseback calling back his two dogs who had made a dash for the kitten. And the silly kitten, instead of running away, froze on the spot, hunched its back, and glared at the dogs. When she saw the dogs, Katya screamed and ran away. But Vasya rushed toward the kitten and got to it at the same instant as the dogs. The dogs were about to grab the poor kitten when Vasya fell on it, protecting it with his body.

The hunter galloped up and drove the dogs away. Vasya took the kitten home. He never again brought it with him to play on the road.

# The Watchman's Dog

There once lived a watchman who had a wife and two children. One day, as the watchman was leaving to go to work, he told his wife not to let their children out of the house, because wolves had prowled near the house during the night and had harassed their dog.

"Children, stay out of the forest," the wife said. Then she went about her work.

While the mother was busy, the brother said to his sister, "Let's go to the forest. Yesterday I saw an apple tree there. It had ripe apples."

"All right, let's go," said the little girl. And off they went.

When their mother finished her work, she called the children, but they weren't in the house. She went out on the porch and called their names loudly. The children were gone!

When her husband came home for supper, he asked, "Where are the children?"
His wife said that she didn't know.

The watchman ran out to look for them. Suddenly he heard the yelping of their dog. He ran into the forest and soon found his children. They were huddled under a bush, crying. Near them a wolf and their dog were locked in fierce battle. The wolf bit the dog again and again. The watchman swung his ax and killed the wolf. Then he lifted the children in his arms and carried them home.

When the whole family was inside the house, the mother bolted the door, and they sat down to eat. Soon they heard the dog whining at the door. They opened it to let her in, but she was covered with blood and couldn't move. The children brought the dog some bread and water. She didn't touch the food or the drink but kept licking their hands lovingly. Then she turned over on her side and stopped whining. The children thought that the dog had gone to sleep, but she was dead.

# The Jump

A ship had sailed around the world and was on its homeward journey. The weather was calm and everyone was on deck. A large monkey was capering about amidst the crowd, amusing everybody. She tumbled here and there, made silly faces, and aped the people. It was clear that she knew that she was funny and therefore carried on even more.

She jumped over to a twelve-year-old boy, the son of the ship's captain, and snatched his hat from his head, put it on her own, and quickly scampered up the mast. Everyone laughed, and the boy didn't know whether to laugh or be angry.

The monkey perched on the bottom crossbeam of the mast, took off the hat and began to tear it with her teeth and paws. She seemed to be doing it to spite the boy. She pointed at him and made funny faces.

The boy shouted at her and threatened her with his fist, but she kept tearing the hat, doing it even harder. The sailors laughed louder, the boy flushed with anger, threw off his jacket, and went after the monkey on the mast. In an instant he had climbed the rope ladder to the first crossbeam. But just as the boy was about to grab his hat from her, the monkey quickly climbed even higher.

"You won't get away with this," the boy cried out, and climbed after the monkey. The animal lured him on, scrambling still higher, to the top of the high mast.

Up there, holding fast to a rope with one foot, the monkey stretched out her body, extended her long arm, and hung the torn cap on the end of the highest crossbeam. Then she reached the very tip of the mast and sat there making faces, baring her teeth, and enjoying her victory.

There was a space of about six feet between the boy and the end of the crossbeam where his hat was hanging now. To reach it, he would have to let go of both the rope and the mast. He was so upset by now that, forgetting all danger, he stepped onto this highest crossbeam, balancing himself the best he could with his arms.

All the people on deck had been watching the chase between the captain's son and the monkey. But when they saw the boy let go of the rope and step out on the crossbeam, they froze with terror. If he lost his balance and fell to the deck, he would be killed. Or even if he somehow reached the end of the crossbeam and got his hat, it would be hard for him to turn around and get back to the mast.

They were looking on in silence, waiting to see what would happen, when someone in the crowd suddenly cried out in panic. The boy heard the cry, looked down, and teetered.

Just then the captain of the ship, the boy's father, came out of his cabin. He was holding a rifle for shooting seagulls. When he saw his son teetering on the uppermost crossbeam, he at once aimed the gun at him, shouting, "Jump! Jump into the water! Or I'll shoot!"

The boy hesitated, not understanding.

"Jump! One, two . . ."

As soon as his father cried, "three," the boy stepped out and dived into the sea.

Like a cannonball his body hit the water, but before the waves could cover him, twenty brave seamen had jumped from the ship into the sea. Within forty seconds—they seemed like eternity—the body of the boy came to the surface. The seamen grabbed him and brought him back on board.

After a few long minutes water began to come from his mouth and nose, and he began to breathe.

When the captain saw this, he uttered a choked cry, and he hurried away to his cabin so that no one would see him weep.

# The Dew
# on the Grass

When you come to a meadow early on a sunny morning, you will see jewels scattered all over the grass. These jewels glisten in the sun and sparkle in many colors— yellow, red, blue. And when you come nearer and look closer, you will see that the gems are drops of dew which have gathered inside the blades of grass with the sun's rays playing on them.

The inside of each blade is mossy and downy, like velvet, and the dewdrops roll over them without wetting them. If you happen to pluck a blade with a dewdrop still cradled in it, the dewdrop will roll off like a tiny ball of light.

Or, maybe you will tear off the little cupful, carefully raise it to your lips and drink the dewdrop. You will think it the most delicious drink in the world.

# FABLES AND
# FAIRY TALES

# What the Little Mouse
# Saw on Her Walk

Little Mouse went for a walk one day. She walked around the barnyard and came home to her mother.

"Mamma," she said, "I saw two animals. One was scary, but the other was nice."

"Tell me," said Mother Mouse, "what kind of animals were they?"

Said Little Mouse, "One struts about the barnyard like this—his legs are black, his comb is red, his eyes bulge, and his nose is hooked. When I passed him, he opened his jaw, raised one leg, and screamed so loudly that I didn't know what to do, I was so frightened!"

"That was the rooster," said Mother Mouse. "He never harms anyone. You needn't be afraid of him. Now tell me about the other animal."

Little Mouse said, "The other lies quietly, warming himself in the sun. He has a sweet little white neck, pretty little paws—gray and soft—and he lies there on his white tummy, flicking his tail. And he winked at me!"

"Silly Little Mouse," said Mother Mouse. "That was the CAT!"

# The Squirrel and the Wolf

A squirrel was leaping from branch to branch and, BOOM! She fell down on a wolf dozing under the tree.

The wolf jumped up, grabbed the squirrel, and was about to gobble her up.

"Don't eat me," begged the squirrel. "Let me go, wolf."

"All right," said the wolf, "I'll let you go if you tell me what makes you squirrels so happy. I am always sad, but whenever I look at you, there you are, up in the tree, playing and capering about."

Then the squirrel said to the wolf, "First let me go back to my tree. I'll tell you from up there, for I'm afraid of you."

The wolf let the squirrel go. She scampered up to a high branch and answered the wolf from there:

"You are always sad because you are mean. Your meanness turns your heart to stone. We squirrels are happy because we are kind and do harm to no one."

# The Hen and Her Chicks

A hen hatched some chicks, but she didn't know how to take care of them. So she said to her chicks, "Crawl back into your shells. I'll sit on you as before and take care of you that way."

The chicks obeyed their mother—they tried to get back into their shells. But they couldn't do it and only crushed their little wings.

Then one of the chicks said to the mother, "If you now want us to stay in our shells all the time, you shouldn't have hatched us."

# The Bat

Long, long ago, there was a fierce war between the beasts and the birds. The Bat didn't join either side, waiting to see who would be the victor.

First the birds defeated the beasts. The Bat then joined them. It flew with them and called itself a bird.

Some time later, when the beasts were about to conquer the birds, the Bat went over to the side of the beasts. It showed them that it too had teeth, paws, and teats. The Bat assured the beasts that it was indeed a beast and that it loved beasts.

In the end the birds won after all. The Bat once more went over to the birds, but they drove it away. Nor would the beasts now let it rejoin them. From that time on the Bat has lived in caves and in the hollows of trees. It flies only after dark, and it belongs neither with the beasts nor with the birds.

# The Fox's Foxy Tail

A man caught a fox and asked her, "Tell me, who taught you foxes to play tricks on the dogs with your tails?"

The fox said, "What do you mean, play tricks? We don't try to fool the dogs, we merely run from them as fast as we can."

"Yes, you do so play tricks with your tails," said the man. "When the dogs catch up with you and are about to seize you, you turn your tail to one side; the dogs make a dash for the tail while you run in the other direction. I've seen it many times with my own eyes."

45

The fox laughed and said, "We don't do this to play tricks on the dogs! We do it so as to turn, fast. You see, man, when the dogs are after us, and we know that we can't save ourselves by running straight ahead, we must run to the side. In order to do this as quickly as possible, we have to swing our tail in the opposite direction. And this isn't something we foxes invented. God thought of it when He created us, so that your dogs wouldn't catch all the foxes in the world."

# The Quail

A quail hatched her baby in the oat field. She worried that the farmer would come to harvest the oats. One day, before flying off to find some food, she said to her children, "Listen carefully to the farmer's talk and tell me what he said when I return."

When the mother quail came back that evening, the baby quails said, "We are in trouble, Mamochka! The farmer was here with his son, and he said, 'The oats are ripe. It is time to do the mowing. Son, go to our neighbors and to our friends and tell them that I would like them to come and help with the mowing.' It isn't safe for us here, Mamochka; take us somewhere else, for early tomorrow they will come to mow the oats."

The mother quail listened to what her children said, and she answered, "Don't worry, my little ones, they won't mow the oats so soon. You are safe here." Again, early next day, the mother quail got ready to leave in search for food. Again she asked her children to listen to what the farmer would say.

The mother quail returned that evening. The little ones said to her, "Well, Mamochka, the farmer was here again. He kept waiting for his friends and neighbors, but no one came. So he said to his son, 'Go to my brothers, to my brothers-in-law, and to our other kin and tell them that your father asks that they come tomorrow without fail to help mow the oat field.' "

"Don't worry, my darlings, tomorrow there will be no mowing either," the mother quail said.

Next day, when the mother quail returned to her children, she asked them, "And what happened today?"

"Again the farmer and his son were here," the little quails said. "They waited and waited for the relatives, but they didn't come. Then the farmer said to his son, 'I guess it's no use waiting for help. The oats are ripe. Let's go at it—tomorrow at dawn we'll come and do our own mowing.' "

The mother quail said, "Well, my children, since the man is going to do his own work and is not waiting any longer for someone else to do it for him, it will now get done. We'd better move!"

# The Two Brothers

Two brothers went on a journey together. At noon one day they lay down for a nap in the forest. When they awoke, they saw a stone lying near them. Something was written on it. Since they hadn't had much schooling, they read the words on the stone with difficulty.

"He who comes upon this stone," they read, "let him go forth into the forest at sunrise. He will come to a river. Let him swim across this river to the opposite bank. There he will see a she-bear with her cubs. Let him take the cubs from the mother and run, without stopping, up the mountain. On top of the mountain he will see a house, and in this house he will find his luck."

When the brothers finished reading what was written on the stone, the younger one said, "Brother, let's go together. Perhaps we'll succeed in swimming across the river. We'll bring the cubs to the house on the mountain, and there we'll find our luck."

Said the older brother, "I will not go into the forest for those cubs, and I advise you not to go either. First of all, no one knows if what is written on the stone is true. Maybe it was written there to fool somebody, or we might not have read the words right. Secondly, even if what is written on the stone *is* true—then, suppose we go into the forest, night falls, we don't find the river and lose our way. And even if we do find the river, how do we know that we can swim across it? The current may be swift and the river may be too wide. Thirdly, even if we do swim across the river safely, there is still the hard task of taking the cubs from the she-bear; she may fall upon us, and instead of finding our luck, we may perish. Fourthly, even if we do carry off the cubs, we cannot reach the summit of the mountain without stopping to rest. But most important, it doesn't say on the stone what kind of luck we will find in the house on top of the mountain. What if we don't want the kind of luck that awaits us there?"

To which the younger brother replied, "I think otherwise. The words on the stone were not written without a purpose. And they were written clearly. First of all, it wouldn't hurt to try. Secondly, if we don't follow the road to our luck, someone else will read what it says on the stone and will find that luck, and we will be left with nothing. Thirdly, without effort and toil, nothing will gladden a man's life. Fourthly, I don't want anyone to think that I was afraid to try."

Then the older brother said, "There is a proverb that says, *look for lots of luck and you may miss even a little luck.* And another proverb says that *a bird in hand is worth two in the bush.*"

50

The younger brother said, "I have heard the saying that *he who fears wolves should stay out of the woods,* and I have also heard the proverb that says, *no water ever flows under a sitting rock.* I think we should go."

The younger brother went but the older one did not.

As soon as the younger brother entered the forest, he saw the river. He swam across it and at once saw the she-bear. He snatched her cubs away from her and ran, without stopping, to the top of the mountain. No sooner did he reach it than people came out of the house to greet him. They brought him a carriage, led him to the city, and made him their king.

He reigned for five years. In the sixth year, a stronger king invaded the land with his army, captured the city, and drove out the ruling king. The younger brother then became a wanderer, and after some time he returned to his older brother.

The older brother had been living all this time in a village. He was neither rich nor poor. The brothers were glad to meet again. They told each other how they had fared.

The older brother said, "You see, I was right. I have lived all this time quietly and fairly well. But although you were a king, you had much trouble because of it."

The younger brother's answer to this was, "I don't regret that I went into the forest that time and up the mountain. It is true that I'm not well-off now, but I have something to remember from the past. But what do you have that is worth remembering?"

# Lipuniushka

There lived an old man and his old wife. They had no children. One day the old man went to the field to plow, while the old woman stayed home to bake him some pancakes. She made a pile of them and said to herself, "If we had a son, he'd take these pancakes to his father. But, as things are, whom will I send?"

Suddenly a tiny boy sprang up from the spinning wheel, saying, "Hello *matushka*, little mother."

"Where did you come from?" asked the old woman, "and what is your name?"

The tiny boy answered, "You, matushka, took a bit of cotton wool, put it around the spindle, and that's how I was born. My name is Lipuniushka. Let me take those pancakes to *batiushka,* to my little father."

"But can you do it, Lipuniushka?"

"I can."

The old woman tied the pancakes in a napkin and gave the bundle to her tiny son. Lipuniushka took it and ran with it to the field. In the field he came to a rock. It was in his way, and he cried, "Batiushka, batiushka, little daddy, little daddy, lift me over the rock! I am bringing you some pancakes."

The old man heard that someone was calling him. He went to the tiny boy and lifted him over the rock. "Where did you come from, sonny?" he asked.

"I was made from a bit of cotton wool. Here are your pancakes."

The old man sat down to eat his breakfast. The tiny boy said, "Batiushka, let me do the plowing while you eat."

"You are not strong enough," said the old man.

"Let me do it, batiushka, let me plow."

And Lipuniushka ran to the plow, grabbed its handles, called to the horse, and set to work. He plowed and sang himself songs.

The old man's master drove by the field. He saw that the old man was sitting, having his breakfast, while the horse was doing the plowing by itself. The master left his carriage and said to the old man, "I see you are letting your horse do your work."

"No, I have a tiny boy there; he works and sings songs."

The master went to the plow, heard the singing, and saw Lipuniushka. He said, "Old man, sell me your tiny boy."

"I can't sell him to you," said the old man. "He is my one and only child!"

Lipuniushka whispered to his father, "Sell me to the master; afterward I'll run away from him."

The old man sold the tiny boy for a hundred rubles.

The master paid the money, picked up Lipuniushka, wrapped him in a handkerchief, and put him in his pocket. When he got home, he said to his wife, "I brought you a darling little thing."

"Show it to me," said the wife.

The master reached for the handkerchief in his pocket, unfolded it, but there was nothing in it. Lipuniushka had long since returned to his father.

# AFTERWORD

The twenty-two stories and fables in this volume were written by the most remarkable Russian man of letters. It is not generally known that Leo Tolstoy, the master of the Russian novel, author of the monumental *War and Peace*, and one of the most revered humanitarians of our times, was also a major children's author.

He wrote several hundred stories, fables, fairy tales and realistic animal tales for the child learning to read. He wrote many of them for his *New Alphabet*, a first reader, and for four graded *Books for Reading*.

The selections in this little volume were chosen from these readers and they include almost every genre of his tales. Two of them, "The Bat" and "The Watchman's Dog," were published posthumously, in the Soviet Union. All the selections offered in this book have been published for the contemporary Russian child.

Tolstoy's interest in the schooling of the small child began when he was still a young man and a bachelor—he subsequently fathered thirteen children. During his travels on the continent, where he went in order to learn about advanced methods of education, he was deeply impressed with the theories of early childhood education of the French philosopher Jean Jacques Rousseau. Tolstoy returned to his country with a plan for opening a school for the peasant children on his estate.

It was during the years when he administered and taught in his school that Tolstoy conceived the idea of his *New Alphabet*. Good readers for the culturally deprived Russian children were nonexistent. Tolstoy was determined to provide such children with good reading material. He set to work and for the next fourteen